The Midnight Heir

A MAGNUS BANE STORY

The Midnight Heir

A MAGNUS BANE STORY

By Cassandra Clare
and Sarah Rees Brennan

WALKER
BOOKS

First published in Great Britain 2013 by Walker Books Ltd
87 Vauxhall Walk, London SE11 5HJ

This edition published 2017

2 4 6 8 10 9 7 5 3

Text © 2013 Cassandra Claire LLC
Previously published in *The Bane Chronicles* and as an individual eBook
Cover illustration © 2017 Dan Funderburgh

The right of Cassandra Clare to be identified as author of this
work has been asserted by her in accordance with the
Copyright, Designs and Patents Act 1988

This book has been typeset in Dolly

Printed and bound by CPI Group (UK) Ltd, Croydon CR0 4YY

British Library Cataloguing in Publication Data:
a catalogue record for this book is available from the British Library

ISBN 978-1-4063-7960-0

www.walker.co.uk

A loud explosion caused him to look up. There was a boy standing in the middle of the room, a cocked silver pistol in his hand. He was surrounded by broken glass, having just shot off one arm of the chandelier.

It took Magnus nearly twenty minutes to notice the boy shooting out all the lights in the room, but to be fair, he had been distracted by the décor.

It had been nearly a quarter century since Magnus had been in London. He had missed the place. Certainly New York had an energy at the turn of the century that no other city could match. Magnus loved being in a carriage rattling into the dazzling lights of Longacre Square, pulling up outside the Olympia Theatre's elaborate French Renaissance facade, or rubbing elbows with a dozen different kinds of people at the hot dog festival in Greenwich Village. He enjoyed traveling on the elevated railways, squealing brakes and all, and he was much looking forward to traveling through the vast underground systems they were building below the very heart of the city. He had seen the construction of the great station at Columbus Circle just before he had left, and hoped to return to find it finished at last.

But London was London, wearing its history in layers, with every age contained in the new age. Magnus had history here too. Magnus had loved people here, and hated them. There had been one woman whom he had both loved and hated, and he had fled London to escape that memory. He sometimes wondered if he had been wrong to leave, if he should have endured the bad memories for the sake of the good, and suffered, and stayed.

Magnus slouched down in the tufted velvet chair—shabby at the arms, worn by decades of sleeves rubbing away the fabric—and gazed around the room. There was a gentility to English places that America, in all her brash youthfulness, could not match. Glimmering chandeliers dripped from the ceiling—cut glass, of course, not crystal, but it shed a pretty light—and electric sconces lined the walls. Magnus still found electricity rather thrilling, though it was duller than witchlight.

Groups of gentlemen sat at tables, playing rounds of faro and piquet. Ladies who were no better than they should be, whose dresses were too tight and too bright and too all the things Magnus liked most, lounged on velvet-covered benches along the walls. Gentlemen who had done well at the tables approached them, flushed with victory and pound notes; those whom Lady Luck had not smiled on drew on their coats at the door and slunk off silently into the night, bereft of money and companionship.

It was all very dramatic, which Magnus enjoyed.

He had not yet grown tired of the pageantry of ordinary life and ordinary people, despite the passage of time and the fact that people were all very much the same in the end.

A loud explosion caused him to look up. There was a boy standing in the middle of the room, a cocked silver pistol in his hand. He was surrounded by broken glass, having just shot off one arm of the chandelier.

Magnus was overwhelmed with the feeling the French called déjà vu, the feeling that *I have been here before*. He had, of course, been in London before, twenty-five years past.

This boy's face was a face to recall the past. This *was* a face from the past, one of the most beautiful faces Magnus could ever recall seeing. It was a face so finely cut that it cast the shabbiness of this place into stark relief—a beauty that burned so fiercely that it put the glare of the electric lights to shame. The boy's skin was so white and clear that it seemed to have a light shining behind it. The lines of his cheekbones, his jaw, and his throat—exposed by a linen shirt open at the collar—were so clean and perfect that he almost would have looked like a statue were it not for the much disheveled and slightly curling hair falling into his face, as black as midnight against his lucent pallor.

The years drew Magnus back again, the fog and gaslight of a London more than twenty years lost rising to claim Magnus. He found his lips shaping a name: Will. Will Herondale.

Magnus stepped forward instinctively, the movement feeling as if it were not of his own volition.

The boy's eyes went to him, and a shock passed through Magnus. They were not Will's eyes, the eyes Magnus remembered being as *blue as a night sky in Hell*, eyes Magnus had seen both despairing and tender.

This boy had shining golden eyes, like a crystal glass filled brimful with crisp white wine and held up to catch the light of a blazing sun. If his skin was luminous, his eyes were radiant. Magnus could not imagine these eyes as tender. The boy was very, very lovely, but his was a beauty like that Helen of Troy might have had once, disaster written in every line. The light of his beauty made Magnus think of cities burning.

Fog and gaslight receded into memory. His momentary lapse into foolish nostalgia was over. This was not Will. That broken, beautiful boy would be a man now, and this boy was a stranger.

Still, Magnus did not think that such a great resemblance could be a coincidence. He made his way toward the boy with little effort, as the other denizens of the gaming hell seemed, perhaps understandably, reluctant to approach him. The boy was standing alone as though the broken glass all around him were a shining sea and he were an island.

"Not precisely a Shadowhunter weapon," Magnus murmured. "Is it?"

Those golden eyes narrowed into bright slits, and the long-fingered hand not holding the pistol went to the boy's sleeve, where Magnus presumed his nearest blade was concealed. His hands were not quite steady.

"Peace," Magnus added. "I mean you no harm. I am a warlock the Whitelaws of New York will vouch for as being quite—well, mostly—harmless."

There was a long pause that felt somewhat dangerous. The boy's eyes were like stars, shining but giving no clue to his feelings. Magnus was generally good at reading people, but he found it difficult to predict what this boy might do.

Magnus was truly surprised by what the boy said next.

"I know who you are." His voice was not like his face; it had gentleness to it.

Magnus managed to hide his surprise and raised his eyebrows in silent inquiry. He had not lived three hundred years without learning not to rise to every bait offered.

"You are Magnus Bane."

Magnus hesitated, then inclined his head. "And you are?"

"I," the boy announced, "am James Herondale."

"You know," Magnus murmured, "I rather thought you might be called something like that. I am delighted to hear that I am famous."

"You're my father's warlock friend. He would always speak of you to my sister and me whenever other Shadowhunters spoke slightingly of Downworlders in our presence. He would say he knew a warlock who was a better friend, and more worth trusting, than many a Nephilim warrior."

The boy's lips curled as he said it, and he spoke mockingly but with more contempt than amusement behind the mockery, as if his father had been a fool to tell him this, and James himself was a fool to repeat it.

Magnus found himself in no mood for cynicism.

They had parted well, he and Will, but he knew Shadowhunters. The Nephilim were swift to judge and condemn a Downworlder for ill deeds, acting as if every sin were graven in stone for all time, proving that Magnus's people were evil by nature. Shadowhunters' conviction of their own angelic virtue and righteousness made it easy for them to let a warlock's good deeds slip their minds, as if they were written in water.

He had not expected to see or hear of Will Herondale on this journey, but if Magnus had thought of it, he would have been unsurprised to be all but forgotten, a petty player in a boy's tragedy. Being remembered, and remembered so kindly, touched him more than he would have thought possible.

The boy's star-shining, burning-city eyes traveled across Magnus's face and saw too much.

"I would not set any great store by it. My father trusts a great many people," James Herondale said, and laughed. It was quite clear suddenly that he was extremely drunk. Not that Magnus had imagined he was firing at chandeliers while stone-cold sober. "Trust. It is like placing a blade in someone's hand and setting the very point against your own heart."

"I have not asked you to trust me," Magnus pointed out mildly. "We have just met."

"Oh, I'll trust you," the boy told him carelessly. "It hardly matters. We are all betrayed sooner or later—all betrayed, or traitors."

"I see that a flair for the dramatic runs in the blood,"

Magnus said under his breath. It was a different kind of dramatics, though. Will had made an exhibition of vice in private, to drive away those nearest and dearest to him. James was making a public spectacle.

Perhaps he loved vice for vice's own sake.

"What?" James asked.

"Nothing," said Magnus. "I was merely wondering what the chandelier had done to offend you."

James looked up at the ruined chandelier, and down at the shards of glass at his feet, as if he were noticing them only now.

"I was bet," he said, "twenty pounds that I would not shoot out all the lights of the chandelier."

"And who bet you?" said Magnus, not divulging a hint of what he thought—that anyone who bet a drunk seventeen-year-old boy that he could wave around a deadly weapon with impunity ought to be in gaol.

"That fellow there," James announced, pointing.

Magnus looked in the general direction James was gesturing toward, and spied a familiar face at the faro table.

"The green one?" Magnus inquired. Coaxing drunken Shadowhunters into making fools of themselves was a favorite occupation among the Downworlders, and this performance had been a tremendous success. Ragnor Fell, the High Warlock of London, shrugged, and Magnus sighed inwardly. Perhaps gaol would be a bit extreme, though Magnus still felt his emerald friend could use taking down a peg or two.

"Is he *really* green?" James asked, not seeming to care overmuch. "I thought that was the absinthe."

Then James Herondale, son of William Herondale and Theresa Gray, the two Shadowhunters who had been the closest of their kind to friends that Magnus had ever known—though Tessa had not been quite a Shadowhunter, or not entirely—turned his back on Magnus, set his sights on a woman serving drinks to a table surrounded by werewolves, and shot her down. She collapsed on the floor with a cry, and all the gamblers sprang from their tables, cards flying and drinks spilling.

James laughed, and the laugh was clear and bright, and it was then that Magnus began to be truly alarmed. Will's voice would have shaken, betraying that his cruelty had been part of his playacting, but his son's laugh was that of someone genuinely delighted by the chaos erupting all around him.

Magnus's hand shot out and grasped the boy's wrist, the hum and light of magic crackling along his fingers like a promise. "That's enough."

"Be easy," James said, still laughing. "I am a very good shot, and Peg the tavern maid is famous for her wooden

$J876522$

leg. I think that is why they call her Peg. Her real name, I believe, is Ermentrude."

"And I suppose Ragnor Fell bet you twenty pounds that you couldn't shoot her without managing to draw blood? How very clever of you both."

James drew his hand back from Magnus's, shaking his head. His black locks fell around a face so like his father's that it prompted an indrawn breath from Magnus. "My father told me you acted as a sort of protector to him, but I do not need your protection, warlock."

"I rather disagree with that."

"I have taken a great many bets tonight," James Herondale informed him. "I must perform all the terrible deeds I have promised. For am I not a man of my word? I want to preserve my honor. And I want another drink!"

"What an excellent idea," Magnus said. "I have heard alcohol only improves a man's aim. The night is young.

Imagine how many barmaids you can shoot before dawn."

"A warlock as dull as a scholar," said James, narrowing his amber eyes. "Who would have thought such a thing existed?"

"Magnus has not always been so dull," said Ragnor, appearing at James's shoulder with a glass of wine in hand. He gave it to the boy, who took it and downed it in a distressingly practiced manner. "There was a time, in Peru, with a boat full of pirates—"

James wiped his mouth on his sleeve and set down his glass. "I should love to sit and listen to old men reminiscing about their lives, but I have a pressing appointment to do something that is actually interesting. Another time, chaps."

He turned upon his heel and left. Magnus made to follow him.

"Let the Nephilim control their brat, if they can,"

Ragnor said, always happy to see chaos but not be involved in it. "Come have a drink with me."

"Another night," Magnus promised.

"Still such a soft touch, Magnus," Ragnor called after him. "Nothing you like better than a lost soul or a bad idea."

Magnus wanted to argue with that, but it was difficult when he was already forsaking warmth and the promise of a drink and a few rounds of cards, and running out into the cold after a deranged Shadowhunter.

Said deranged Shadowhunter turned on him, as if the narrow cobbled street were a cage and he some wild, hungry animal held there too long.

"I wouldn't follow me," James warned. "I am in no mood for company. Especially the company of a prim magical chaperone who does not know how to enjoy himself."

"I know perfectly well how to enjoy myself," remarked Magnus, amused, and he made a small gesture so that for an instant all the iron streetlamps lining the street rained down varicolored sparks of light. For an instant he thought he saw a light that was softer and less like burning in James Herondale's golden eyes, the beginnings of a childlike smile of delight.

The next moment, it was quenched. James's eyes were as bright as the jewels in a dragon's hoard, and no more alive or joyful. He shook his head, black locks flying in the night air, where the magic lights were fading.

"But you do not wish to enjoy yourself, do you, James Herondale?" Magnus asked. "Not really. You want to go to the devil."

"Perhaps I think I will enjoy going to the devil," said James Herondale, and his eyes burned like the fires of Hell, enticing, and promising unimaginable suffering.

"Though I see no need to take anyone else with me."

No sooner had he spoken than he vanished, to all appearances softly and silently stolen away by the night air, with no one but the winking stars, the glaring streetlamps, and Magnus as witnesses.

Magnus knew magic when he saw it. He spun, and at the same moment heard the click of a decided footstep against a cobblestone. He turned to face a policeman walking his beat, truncheon swinging at his side, and a look of suspicion on his stolid face as he surveyed Magnus.

It was not Magnus the man had to watch out for.

Magnus saw the buttons on the man's uniform cease their gleaming, even though he was under a streetlamp. Magnus was able to discern a shadow falling where there was nothing to cast it, a surge of dark within the greater darkness of the night.

The policeman gave a shout of surprise as his helmet was whisked away by unseen hands. He stumbled forward, hands fumbling blindly in the air to retrieve what was long gone.

Magnus gave him a consoling smile. "Cheer up," he said. "You can find far more flattering headgear at any shop in Bond Street."

The man fainted. Magnus considered pausing to help him, but there was being a soft touch, and then there was being ridiculous enough to not pursue a most enticing mystery. A Shadowhunter who could turn into a shadow? Magnus turned and bolted after the bobbing policeman's helmet, held aloft only by a taunting darkness.

They ran down street after street, Magnus and the darkness, until the Thames barred their path. Magnus heard the sound of its rushing swiftness rather than saw it, the dark waters at one with the night.

What he did see was white fingers suddenly clenched on the brim of the policeman's helmet, the turn of James Herondale's head, darkness replaced with the tilt of his slowly appearing grin. Magnus saw a shadow coalescing once more into flesh.

So the boy had inherited something from his mother as well as his father, then. Tessa's father had been a fallen angel, one of the kings of demons. The boy's lambent golden eyes seemed to Magnus like his own eyes suddenly, a token of infernal blood.

James saw Magnus looking, and winked before he hurled the helmet up into the air. It flew for a moment like a strange bird, spinning gently around in the air, then hit the water. The darkness was disrupted by a silver splash.

"A Shadowhunter who knows magic tricks," Magnus observed. "How novel."

A Shadowhunter who attacked the mundanes it was his mandate to protect—how delighted the Clave would be by that.

"We are but dust and shadows, as the saying goes," said James. "Of course, the saying does not add, 'Some of us also turn into shadows occasionally, when the mood takes us.' I suppose nobody predicted that I would come to pass. It's true that I have been told I am somewhat unpredictable."

"May I ask who bet you that you could steal a policeman's helmet, and why?"

"Foolish question. Never ask about the last bet, Bane," James advised him, and reached casually to his belt, where his gun was slung, and then he drew it in one fluid, easy motion. "You should be worrying about the next one."

"There isn't any chance," Magnus asked, without much

hope, "that you are rather a nice fellow who believes he is cursed and must make himself seem unlovable to spare those around him from a terrible fate? Because I have heard that happens sometimes."

James seemed amused by the question. He smiled, and as he smiled, his waving black locks blended with the night, and the glow of his skin and his eyes grew as distant as the light of the stars until they became so pale, they diffused. He was nothing but a shadow among shadows again. He was an infuriating Cheshire cat of a boy, nothing left of him but the impression of his smile.

"My father was cursed," James said from the darkness. "Whereas I? I'm damned."

The London Institute was exactly as Magnus remembered it, tall and white and imposing, its tower cutting a white line against the dark sky. Shadowhunter

Institutes were built as monuments to withstand the ravages of demons and time. When the doors opened, Magnus beheld again the massive stone entryway and the two flights of stairs.

A woman with wildly curling red hair, whom Magnus was sure he should remember but didn't, answered the door, her face creased with sleep and crossness. "What d'you want, warlock?" she demanded.

Magnus shifted the burden in his arms. The boy was tall, and Magnus had had a long night besides. Annoyance made his tone rather sharp as he answered:

"I want you to go tell Will Herondale that I have brought his whelp home."

The woman's eyes widened. She gave an impressed sort of whistle and vanished abruptly. A handful of moments later Magnus saw a white figure come softly down one of the staircases.

Tessa was like the Institute: hardly changed at all. She had the same smooth youthful face that she had worn twenty-five years before. Magnus thought she must have stopped aging no more than three or four years after he had last seen her. Her hair was in a long brown plait, hanging over one shoulder, and she was holding a witchlight in one hand and had a small sphere of light shining in her palm in the other.

"Been taking magic lessons, have we, Tessa?" Magnus asked.

"Magnus!" Tessa exclaimed, and her grave face lit with a welcoming smile that sent a pang of sweetness through Magnus. "But they said— Oh, no. Oh, where did you find Jamie?"

She reached the bottom of the steps, went over to Magnus, and cradled the boy's damp head in her hand in an almost absentminded gesture of affection. In that gesture Magnus saw how she had changed, saw the ingrained habit of motherhood, love for someone she had created and whom she cherished.

No other warlock would ever have a child of their own blood. Only Tessa could have that experience.

Magnus turned his head away from Tessa at the sound of a new footfall on the stairs.

The memory of Will the boy was so fresh that it was something of a shock to see Will himself now, older, broader of shoulder, but still with the same tousled black hair and laughing blue eyes. He looked just as handsome as he had ever been—more so perhaps, since he seemed so much happier. Magnus saw more marks of laughter than of time on his face, and found himself smiling. It was true what Will had said, he realized. They were friends.

Recognition crossed Will's face, and with it pleasure,

but almost instantly he saw the burden Magnus carried, and worry erased all else.

"Magnus," he said. "What on earth happened to James?"

"What happened?" Magnus asked musingly. "Well, let me see. He stole a bicycle and rode it, not using his hands at any point, through Trafalgar Square. He attempted to climb Nelson's Column and fight with Nelson. Then I lost him for a brief period of time, and by the time I caught up with him, he had wandered into Hyde Park, waded into the Serpentine, spread his arms wide, and was shouting, 'Ducks, embrace me as your king!'"

"Dear God," said Will. "He must have been vilely drunk. Tessa, I can bear it no longer. He is taking awful risks with his life and rejecting all the principles I hold most dear. If he continues making an exhibition of himself throughout London, he will be called to Idris and kept there away from the mundanes. Does he not realize that?"

Magnus shrugged. "He also made inappropriate amorous advances to a startled grandmotherly sort selling flowers, an Irish wolfhound, an innocent hat stand in a dwelling he broke into, and myself. I will add that I do not believe his admiration of my person, dazzling though I am, to be sincere. He told me I was a beautiful, sparkling lady. Then he abruptly collapsed, naturally in the path of an oncoming train from Dover, and I decided it was well past time to take him home and place him in the bosom of his family. If you had rather I put him in an orphanage, I fully understand."

Will was shaking his head, shadows in his blue eyes now. "Bridget," he shouted, and Magnus thought, *Oh, yes, that was the maid's name.* "Call for the Silent Brothers," Will finished.

"You mean call for Jem," Tessa said, dropping her voice, and she and Will shared a look—what Magnus could describe only as a *married* look, the look of two people who understood each other completely and yet found each other adorable all the same.

It was quite sickening.

He cleared his throat. "Still a Silent Brother, then, is he?"

Will gave Magnus a withering look. "It does tend to be a permanent state. Here, give me my son."

Magnus let Will take James from his arms, which were left lighter if more damp, and Magnus followed Will's and Tessa's lead up the stairs. Inside the Institute it was clear they had been redecorating. Charlotte's dark drawing room now held several comfortable-looking sofas, and the walls were covered in light damask. Tall shelves were lined with books, volumes with the gilt rubbed off their spines and, Magnus was sure, the pages much thumbed. It appeared both Tessa and Will remained great readers.

Will deposited James onto one of the sofas. Tessa rushed to find a blanket as Magnus turned toward the door, only to find his hand caught in Will's grasp.

"It was very good of you to bring Jamie home," Will said. "But you were always so good to me and mine. I was little more than a boy then, and not as grateful or as gracious as I should have been."

"You were well enough, Will," said Magnus. "And I see you have grown to be better. Also, you are not bald, and neither have you grown fat. All that dashing about and fighting evil you people do is at least useful for keeping a trim figure in middle age."

Will laughed. "It's very good to see you, too." He hesitated. "About Jamie..."

Magnus tensed. He had not wanted to distress Will and Tessa too much. He had not told them that James had fallen when he was in the Serpentine, and made very little effort to rescue himself from drowning. He had not seemed to want to be taken from the cold depths of the water: had fought Magnus as he dragged him out, then laid his pale cheek against the dank earth of the riverbank and hid his face in his arms.

For a moment Magnus had thought he was crying, but as he stooped down to check on the boy, he found he was barely conscious. With his cruel golden eyes closed, he once again reminded Magnus of the lost boy Will had been. Magnus touched his damp hair gently and said "James," in as kind a voice as he could.

The boy's pale hands were splayed against the dark earth. The glimmer of the Herondale ring shone against his skin, and the edge of something metallic shone under his sleeve as well. His eyes were shut, the black lashes ink-dark crescents against the lines of his cheekbones. Sparkling drops of water were caught in the curling ends of those lashes, which made him look unhappy in a way he did not when awake.

"*Grace*," James had whispered in his sleep, and was silent.

Magnus had not been angry: he had found himself wishing for a benevolent grace many times himself. He bent and gathered the boy up in his arms. His head lolled against Magnus's shoulder. In sleep James had looked peaceful and innocent, and wholly human.

"This just isn't like him," Will was saying now as Tessa drew a blanket up over the boy, tucking him in firmly.

Magnus raised an eyebrow. "He's *your* son."

"What are you trying to imply?" Will demanded, and for a moment Magnus saw his eyes flash, and saw the boy with messy black hair and glaring blue eyes standing in his drawing room, furious at the whole world and at no part of it more than himself.

"It isn't like him," Tessa agreed. "He's always been so quiet, so studious. Lucie was the impetuous one, but they are both kind, good-hearted children. At parties Jamie could most often be found curled up in a corner with his Latin, or laughing at a private joke with his *parabatai*. He always kept Matthew out of trouble as well as himself. He was the only one who could make that indolent boy attend to his studies," she remarked, with a slight smile that betokened she was fond of her son's *parabatai*, no matter what his faults. "Now he is out at all hours, doing the most disgraceful things, and he will not listen to reason. He will not listen to anybody. I understand what you mean about Will, but Will was lonely and wretched in the days when he behaved badly. James has been wrapped in love all his life."

"Betrayed!" Will muttered. "Cruelly maligned by my friend and now by my own cherished wife, scorned, my name blackened—"

"I see you are still fond of histrionics, Will," said Magnus. "As well as still handsome."

They had grown up. Neither of them looked startled at all. Tessa raised her eyebrows, and Magnus saw something of her son in her then. They both had the same expressive, arched brows, giving their faces a look of both inquiry and amusement, though in James's face the amusement was bitter.

"Do stop flirting with my husband," said Tessa.

"I shall not," Magnus declared, "but I will pause briefly so that I may catch up on your news. I have not heard from you since you sent word the baby had arrived and both he and his lovely mother were thriving."

Will looked surprised. "But we sent you several letters

in care of the Morgensterns, who were going to visit the Whitelaws at the New York Institute. It was you who proved to be a shocking correspondent."

"Ah," said Magnus. He himself was not even slightly surprised. This was typical behavior from Shadowhunters. "The Morgensterns must have forgotten to deliver them. How careless."

Tessa, he saw, did not look too surprised either. She was both warlock and Shadowhunter, and yet not quite either. The Shadowhunters believed that Shadowhunter blood trumped all else, but Magnus could well believe that many of the Nephilim might be unkind to a woman who could do magic and whom the years did not touch.

He doubted any of them dared be unkind in front of Will, though.

"We will be more careful about whom we entrust with our letters in future," Tessa said decisively. "We have been out of touch for far too long. How fortunate that you are here in London, both for us and for Jamie. What brings you here, business or pleasure?"

"I wish it were the business of pleasure," Magnus told her. "But no, it is very dull. A Shadowhunter I believe you know sent for me—Tatiana Blackthorn? The lady used to be a Lightwood, did she not?" Magnus turned to Will. "And your sister Cecily married her brother. Gilbert. Gaston. I have a shocking memory for Lightwoods."

"I begged Cecily not to throw herself away on a Lightworm," Will muttered.

"Will!" said Tessa. "Cecily and Gabriel are very happy together."

Will threw himself dramatically into an armchair, touching his son's wrist as he passed by, with a light, careful caress that spoke volumes.

"At least you must admit, Tess, that Tatiana is as mad

as a mouse trapped in a teapot. She refuses to speak to any of us, and that includes her brothers, because she says we had a hand in her father's death. Actually, she says we pitilessly slew him. Everybody tries to point out that at the time of the pitiless slaying her father was a giant worm who had eaten her husband and followed up his meal with a palate-cleansing servant sorbet, but she insists on lurking about the manor house and sulking with all the curtains drawn."

"She has lost a great deal. She lost her child," Tessa said. "And she did speak to us that once, in Idris." She stroked back her son's hair, her face troubled. Will looked to James and fell silent.

"Mrs. Blackthorn has come from Idris to her family manor in England specifically so I might visit her, and she sent me a message through the usual Downworlder channels promising me a princely sum if I would come and cast a few spells to increase the attractions of her young ward," Magnus said, attempting to strike a lighter note. "I gather she wishes to marry her off."

Tatiana would not be the first Shadowhunter to seek a warlock's spells to make her life easier and more pleasant. She was, however, the Shadowhunter offering the best price.

"Did she?" Will asked. "It's not as if the girl looks like a toad in a bonnet."

Tessa laughed and stifled the laugh against her hand, and Will grinned, looking pleased with himself, as he always had when he'd managed to amuse Tessa.

"I suppose I should not be casting aspersions on anybody else's children, since my son is all about in his wits. He shoots things, you know."

"I did know that he shoots things," Magnus said tactfully. "Yes."

Will sighed. "The Angel grant me patience so I do not strangle him, and wisdom so I can talk some sense into his great fat head."

"I do wonder where he gets it from," said Magnus pointedly.

"It is not the same," said Tessa. "When Will was Jamie's age, he tried to drive everyone he loved away. Jamie is as loving as ever to us, to Lucie, to Matthew, his *parabatai*. It is himself he wishes to destroy."

"And yet there is no reason for it," Will said, striking the arm of his chair with his clenched fist. "I know my son, and he would not behave this way unless he felt he had no other choice. Unless he was trying to achieve a goal, or punish himself in some way, because he felt he had done some wrong—"

You called for me? I am here.

Magnus looked up to see Brother Zachariah standing in

the doorway. He was a slender outline, the hood of his robe down, baring his face. The Silent Brothers rarely bared their faces, knowing how most Shadowhunters reacted to the scars and disfigurement of their skin. It was a sign of trust that Jem showed himself to Will and Tessa in this way.

Jem was still Jem—like Tessa, he had not aged. The Silent Brothers were not immortal but aged incredibly slowly. The powerful runes that gave them knowledge and allowed them to speak with their minds also slowed their bodies' aging, turning the Brothers to living statues. Jem's hands were pale and slender under the cuffs of his robe, still musician's hands after all this time. His face seemed carved out of marble, his eyes shuttered crescents, the dark runes of the Brothers standing out on his high cheekbones. His hair waved around his temples, darkness shot with silver.

A great sadness welled up in Magnus at the sight of him. It was human to age and die, and Jem stood outside that humanity now, outside the light that burned so brightly and so briefly. It was cold outside that light and fire. No one had greater cause to know that cold than Magnus did.

On seeing Magnus, Jem inclined his head. *Magnus Bane. I did not know you would be here.*

"I—" Magnus began, but Will was already on his feet, striding across the room to Jem. He had lit up at the sight of him, and Magnus could feel Jem's attention move from himself to Will, and catch there. Those two boys had been so different, yet at times they had seemed so wholly one that it was strange for Magnus to see Will changed as all humans changed, while Jem was set apart, to see that both had gone somewhere the other could not follow. He imagined it must be even stranger for them.

And yet. There was still about them what had always reminded Magnus of an old legend he'd heard of the red thread of fate: that an invisible scarlet thread bound certain people, and however tangled it became, it could not and would not break.

The Silent Brothers moved the way one imagined a statue would move if it could. Jem had moved the same way coming in, but as Will neared him, Jem took a step toward his former *parabatai*, and the step was swift, eager, and human, as if being close to the people whom he loved made him feel made of flesh and racing blood once more.

"You're here," said Will, and implicit in the words was the sense that Will's contentment was complete. Now Jem was there, all was right with the world.

"I knew you would come," said Tessa, rising from her son's side to go after her husband, toward Jem. Magnus saw Brother Zachariah's face glow at the sound of her voice, runes and pallor no longer mattering. He was a boy again for an instant, his life just beginning, his heart full of hope and love.

How they loved each other, these three, how they had suffered for each other, and yet how much joy they clearly took from simply being in the same room. Magnus had loved before, many times, but he did not ever recall feeling the peace that radiated out from these three only from being in the others' presence. He had craved peace sometimes, like a man wandering for centuries in the desert never seeing water and having to live with the want of it.

Tessa, Will, and their lost Jem stood together in a tight knot. Magnus knew that for a few moments nothing existed in the world but the three of them.

He looked at the sofa where James Herondale lay, and saw that he was awake, his gold eyes like watchful flames teaching the candles to burn brightly. James was the young one, the boy with his whole life ahead of him, but there was no hope or joy in his face. Tessa, Will, and Jem looked natural being together, but even in this room with those who loved him better than life, James looked utterly alone. There was something desperate and desolate about his face. He tried to lean up on one elbow, and collapsed back against the cushions of the sofa, his black head tipped back as if it were too heavy for him to bear. A Herondale ring glittered on his finger, a silver bracelet on his wrist.

Tessa, Will, and Jem were murmuring together, Will's hand on Jem's arm. Magnus had never seen anyone touch a Silent Brother like that, in simple friendship. It made him ache inside, and he saw that hollow ache reflected on the face of the boy on the sofa.

Obeying an impetuous impulse, Magnus crossed the

room and knelt down by the couch, close to Will's son, who looked at him with tired golden eyes. "You see them," James said. "The way they all love one another. I used to think everyone loved that way. The way it is in fairy tales. I used to think that love was giving and generous and good."

"And now?" Magnus asked.

The boy turned his face away. Magnus found himself facing the back of James's head, seeing his mop of black hair so like his father's, and the edge of his *parabatai* rune just under his collar. It must be on his back, Magnus thought, above the blade of his shoulder, where an angel's wing would be.

"James," said Magnus in a low, hurried voice. "Once your father had a terrible secret that he thought he could not tell to a soul in the world, and he told me. I can see that there is something gnawing at you, something you are keeping hidden. If there is anything you want to tell me, now or at any time, you have my word that I will keep your secrets, and that I will help you if I can."

James shifted to look at Magnus. In his face Magnus thought he caught a glimpse of softening, as if the boy were releasing his relentless grip on whatever was tormenting him. "I am not like my father," he said. "Do not mistake my despair for nobility in disguise, for it is not that. I suffer for myself, not for anyone else."

"But *why* do you suffer?" Magnus said in frustration. "Your mother was correct when she said you have been loved all your life. If you would just let me help you—"

The boy's expression shut like a door. He turned his face away from Magnus again, and his eyes closed, the light falling on the fringe of his eyelashes.

"I gave my word I would never tell," he said. "And there is not a living soul on this earth who can help me."

"James," Magnus said, honestly surprised by the

despair in the boy's tone, and the alarm in Magnus's voice caught the attention of the others in the room. Tessa and Will looked away from Jem and to their son, the boy who bore Jem's name, and as one they all moved over to where he lay, Will and Tessa hand in hand.

Brother Zachariah bent over the back of the sofa and touched James's hair tenderly with those musician's fingers.

"Hello, Uncle Brother Zachariah," James said without opening his eyes. "I would say that I'm sorry to bother you, but I'm sure this is the most excitement you've had all year. Not so lively in the City of Bones, now is it?"

"James!" Will snapped. "Don't talk to Jem like that."

As if I am not used to badly behaved Herondales, Brother Zachariah said, in the way Jem had always tried to make peace between Will and the world.

"I suppose the difference is that Father always cared

what you thought about him," said James. "And I don't. But don't take it personally, Uncle Jem. I do not care what anybody thinks."

And yet he made a habit of making an exhibition of himself, as Will had put it, and Magnus had no doubt it was deliberate. He must care what someone thought. He must be doing all this for a purpose. *But what purpose could it be?* Magnus wondered.

"James, this is so unlike you," Tessa said worriedly. "You have always cared. Always been kind. What is troubling you?"

"Perhaps nothing is troubling me. Perhaps I have simply realized I was rather boring before. Don't you think I was boring? All that studying, and the Latin." He shuddered. "Horrible."

There is nothing boring about caring, or about an open, loving heart, said Jem.

"So say all of you," replied James. "And it is easy to see why, the three of you, falling over yourself to love one another—each more than the other. And it *is* kind of you to trouble yourselves about me." His breath caught a little, and then he smiled, but it was a smile of great sadness. "I wish I did not trouble you so."

Tessa and Will exchanged looks of despair. The room was thick with worry and parental concerns. Magnus was beginning to feel bowed under by the weight of humanity.

"Well," he announced. "As educational and occasionally damp as this evening has been, I do not wish to intrude on a family reunion, and I really do not wish to experience any family drama, as I find with Shadowhunters that it tends to be extensive. I must be on my way."

"But you could stay here," Tessa offered. "Be our guest. We would be delighted to have you."

"A warlock in the hallowed chambers of a Shadowhunter

Institute?" Magnus shuddered. "Only think."

Tessa gave him a sharp look. "Magnus—"

"Besides, I have an appointment," Magnus said. "One I should not be late for."

Will looked up with a frown. "At this time of night?"

"I have a peculiar occupation, and keep peculiar hours," said Magnus. "I seem to recall you coming to me for assistance quite a few times at odd hours of the night." He inclined his head. "Will. Tessa. Jem. Good evening."

Tessa moved to his side. "I will show you out."

"Good-bye, whoever you are," said James sleepily, closing his eyes. "I cannot recall your name."

"Don't mind him," Tessa said in a low voice as she moved with Magnus toward the exit. She paused in the doorway for a moment, looking back at her son and the two men who stood with him. Will and Jem were shoulder to shoulder, and from across the room it was impossible to miss Jem's slighter frame, the fact that he had not aged, as Will had. Though, there was in Will's voice all the eagerness of a boy when he said, in answer to a question Magnus did not hear, "Why, yes, of course you can play it before you go. It is in the music room as always, kept ever the same for you."

"His violin?" Magnus murmured. "I did not think the Silent Brothers cared for music."

Tessa sighed softly and moved out into the corridor, Magnus beside her. "Will does not see a Silent Brother when he looks at James," she said. "He sees only Jem."

"Is it ever difficult?" he asked.

"Is what difficult?"

"Sharing your husband's heart so entirely with someone else," he said.

"If it were different, it would not be Will's heart," Tessa said. "He knows he shares my heart with Jem as well.

I would have it no other way—and he would have it no other way with me."

So much a part of one another that there was no way to be untangled, even now, and no wish to be so. Magnus wanted to ask if Tessa was ever afraid of what would happen to her when Will was gone, when their bond was finally severed, but he did not. It would with luck be a long time until Tessa's first death, a long time before she entirely realized the burden of being immortal and yet loving that which was not.

"Very beautiful," Magnus said instead. "Well, I wish you all the best with your little hellion."

"We shall see you again before you leave London, of course," said Tessa in that tone of hers she had had even as a girl, that brooked no contradiction.

"Indeed," Magnus said. He hesitated. "And, Tessa, if you ever need me—and I hope if you do, it will be many long, happy years from now—send me a message, and I will be with you at once."

They both knew what he meant.

"I will," said Tessa, and she gave him her hand. Hers was small and soft, but her grip was surprisingly strong.

"Believe me, dear lady," Magnus told her with an assumption of lightness. He released her hand and bowed with a flourish. "Call me and I come!"

As Magnus turned to walk away from the church, he heard the sound of violin music carried to him on the cloudy London air, and remembered another night, a night of ghosts and snow and Christmas music, and Will standing on the steps of the Institute, watching Magnus as he went. Now it was Tessa who stood at the door with her hand lifted in farewell until Magnus was at the gate with its ominous lettered message: WE ARE DUST AND SHADOWS. He looked back and saw her slight pale figure at the Institute threshold and thought again, *Yes, perhaps I was wrong to leave London.*

It was not the first time Magnus had made his way from London to Chiswick to visit Lightwood House. Benedict Lightwood's home had often been thrown open to Downworlders who'd been amenable to his idea of a good time.

It had been a grand manor once, the stone brilliant white and adorned with Greek statuary and too many pillars to count. The Lightwoods were proud and ostentatious people, and their home, in all its neoclassical glory, had reflected that.

Magnus knew what had become of all that pride. The patriarch, Benedict Lightwood, had contracted a disease from consorting with demons and had transformed into a murderous monster that his own sons had been forced to slay, with the assistance of a host of other Shadowhunters. Their manor had been taken away by the Clave as punishment, their monies confiscated, and their family had become a laughingstock, a byword for sin and a betrayal of all that the Shadowhunters held dear.

Magnus had little time for the Shadowhunters' overweening arrogance, and usually enjoyed seeing them taken down a peg, but even he had rarely seen a family fall so far so terribly fast. Gabriel and Gideon, Benedict's two sons, had managed to claw their way back to respectability through good behavior and the graces of the Consul, Charlotte Branwell. Their sister, however, was another matter entirely.

How she had managed to get Lightwood House back into her clutches, Magnus did not know. *As mad as a mouse trapped in a teapot,* Will had said of her, and knowing of the family's disgraced state, Magnus hardly expected the grandeur of Benedict's time. Doubtless the place would be shabby now, dusty with time, only a few servants left to keep it up and in order—

The carriage Magnus had hired came to a stop. "The place looks abandoned," opined the driver, casting a doubtful eye over at the iron gates, which looked rusted shut and bound with vines.

"Or haunted," Magnus suggested brightly.

"Well, I can't get in. Them gates won't open," said the driver gruffly. "You'll have to get out and walk, if you're that determined."

Magnus was. His curiosity was alight now, and he approached the gates like a cat, ready to scale them if need be.

A tweak of magic, a bit of an opening spell, and the gates burst wide with a shower of rusted metal flakes, onto a long, dark overgrown drive that led up to a ghostly manor house in the distance, glimmering like a tombstone under the full moon.

Magnus closed the gates and went forward, listening to the sound of night birds in the trees overhead, the rustle of leaves in the night wind. A forest of blackened tangles loomed all about him, the remains of the famous Lightwood gardens. Those gardens had been lovely once. Magnus distantly recalled overhearing Benedict Lightwood drunkenly saying that they had been his dead wife's joy.

Now the high hedges of the Italian garden had formed a maze, a twisted one from which there was clearly no escape. They had killed the monster Benedict Lightwood had become in these gardens, Magnus remembered hearing, and the black ichor had seeped from the monster's veins into the earth in a dark unstoppable flood.

Magnus felt a scratch against one hand and looked

down to see a rosebush that had survived but gone wild. It took him a moment to identify the plant, for though the shape of the blooms was familiar, the color was not. The roses were as black as the blood of the dead serpent.

He plucked one. The flower crumbled in his palm as if it were made of ash, as if it had already been dead.

Magnus passed on toward the house.

The corruption that had claimed the roses had not spared the manor. What had once been a smooth white facade was now gray with years, streaked with the black of dirt and the green of rot. The shining pillars were twined about with dying vines, and the balconies, which Magnus remembered as like the hollows of alabaster goblets, were now filled with the dark snarls of thorns and the debris of years.

The door knocker had been an image of a shining golden lion with a ring held in its mouth. Now the ring lay rotted on the steps, and the gray lion's mouth hung open and empty in a hungry snarl. Magnus knocked briskly on the door. He heard the sound echo through the inside of the house as if all were the heavy silence of a tomb therein and ever would be, as if any noise was a disturbance.

The conviction that everyone in this house must be dead had gained such a hold on Magnus that it was a shock when the woman who had summoned him here opened the door.

It was, of course, rather odd for a lady to be opening her own front door, but from the look of the place, Magnus assumed the entire staff of servants had been given the decade off.

Magnus had a dim recollection of seeing Tatiana Lightwood at one of her father's parties: a glimpse of a perfectly ordinary girl with wide green eyes, behind a hastily closing door.

Even after seeing the house and the grounds, he was not prepared for Tatiana Blackthorn.

Her eyes were still very green. Her stern mouth was bracketed with lines of bitter disappointment and grave pain. She looked like a woman in her sixties, not her forties. She was wearing a gown of a fashion decades past—it hung from her wasted shoulders and fluttered around her body like a shroud. The fabric bore dark brown stains, but in patches it was a faded pastel bordering on white, while other spots remained what Magnus thought must have been its original fuchsia.

She should have looked ridiculous. She was wearing a silly bright pink dress for a younger woman, someone who was almost a girl, in love with her husband and going on a visit to her papa.

She did not look ridiculous. Her stern face forbade pity. She, like the house, was awe-inspiring in her ruin.

"Bane," Tatiana said, and held the door open wide enough that Magnus could pass through. She said no word of welcome.

She shut the door behind Magnus, the sound as final as the closing of a tomb. Magnus paused in the hall, waiting for the woman behind him, and as he waited, he heard another footstep above their heads, a sign there was someone else alive in the house.

Down the wide curving staircase toward them came a girl. Magnus had always found mortals to be beautiful, and had seen many mortals whom anybody would have described as beautiful.

This was extraordinary beauty, beauty unlike the beauty of most mortals.

In the stained and filthy ruin the house had become, she shone like a pearl. Her hair was the color of a pearl too, palest ivory with a sheen of gold on it, and her skin was the luminous pink and white of a seashell. Her lashes were thick and dark, veiling eyes of deep unearthly gray.

Magnus drew in a breath. Tatiana heard him and looked over, smiling a triumphant smile. "She's glorious, isn't she? My ward. My Grace."

Grace.

The realization struck Magnus like a blow. Of course James Herondale had not been calling out for something as inchoate and distant as a benediction, the soul's yearning for divine mercy and understanding. His desperation had been centered on something far more flesh-and-blood than that.

But why is it a secret? Why can no one help him? Magnus struggled to keep his face a blank as the girl moved toward him and offered her hand.

"How do you do," she murmured.

Magnus stared down at her. Her face was a porcelain

cup, upturned; her eyes held promises. The combination of beauty, innocence, and the promise of sin was staggering. "Magnus Bane," she said, in a breathy, soft voice. Magnus couldn't help staring at her. Everything about her was so perfectly constructed to appeal. She was beautiful, yes, but it was more than that. She seemed shy, yet all her attention was focused on Magnus, as if he were the most fascinating thing she had ever seen. There was no man who did not want to see himself reflected like that in a beautiful girl's eyes. And if the neckline of her dress was a shade low, it did not seem scandalous, for her gray eyes were full of an innocence that said that she did not know of desire, not yet, but there was a lushness to the curve of her lip, a dark light in her eyes that said that under the right hands she would be a pupil who yielded the most exquisite result...

Magnus took a step back from her as if she were a

poisonous snake. She did not look hurt, or angry, or even startled. She turned a look on Tatiana, a sort of curious inquiry. "Mama?" she said. "What is wrong?"

Tatiana curled her lip. "This one is not like others," she said. "I mean, he likes girls well enough, and boys as well, I hear, but his taste does not run to Shadowhunters. And he is not mortal. He has been alive a long time. One cannot expect him to have the normal—reactions."

Magnus could well imagine what the normal reactions would be—the reactions of a boy like James Herondale, sheltered and taught that love was gentle, love was kind, that one should love with all one's heart and give away all one's soul. Magnus could imagine the normal reactions to this girl, a girl whose every gesture, every expression, every line, cried, *Love her, love her, love her.*

But Magnus was not that boy. He reminded himself of his manners, and bowed.

"Charmed," he said. "Or whatever effect would please you best, I'm sure."

Grace regarded him with cool interest. Her reactions were muted, Magnus thought, or rather, carefully gauged. She seemed a creature made to attract everyone and express nothing real, though it would take a master observer, like Magnus, to know it.

She reminded Magnus suddenly not of any mortal but of the vampire Camille, who had been his latest and most regrettable real love.

Magnus had spent years imagining there was fire behind Camille's ice, that there were hopes and dreams and love waiting for him. What he had loved in Camille had been nothing but illusion. Magnus had acted like a child, fancying there were shapes and stories to be made of the clouds in the sky.

He turned away from the sight of Grace in her trim

white-and-blue dress, like a vision of Heaven in the gray hell of this house, and looked to Tatiana. Her eyes were narrowed with contempt.

"Come, warlock," she said. "I believe we have business to discuss."

Magnus followed Tatiana and Grace up the stairs and down a long corridor that was almost pitch black. Magnus heard the crack and crunch of broken glass beneath his feet, and in the dim, hardly-there light he saw something scuttling away from his approach. He hoped it was something as harmless as a rat, but something about its movements suggested a shape far more grotesque.

"Do not try to open any doors or drawers while you are here, Bane." Tatiana's voice floated back to him. "My father left behind many guardians to protect what is ours."

She opened the door, and Magnus beheld the room

within. There were an upturned desk and heavy curtains sagging in the windows like bodies from a gibbet, and on the wooden floor were splinters and streaks of blood, the marks of a long-ago struggle nobody had cleaned up.

There were many picture frames hanging askew or with the glass broken. A great many of them seemed to contain nautical adventures—Magnus had been put off the sea by his ill-fated attempt to live a piratical life for a day—but even the pictures that were whole were clouded with gray. The painted ships appeared to be sinking in seas of dust.

There was only one portrait that was whole and clean. It was an oil painting, with no glass covering it, but there was not a speck of dust on its surface. It was the only clean thing, besides Grace, in the entire house.

The portrait was of a boy, about seventeen years old. He was sitting in a chair, his head resting against the back as if he did not have the strength to support it on his own. He was terribly thin and as white as salt. His eyes were a deep, still green, like a woodland pool hidden under the overhanging leaves of a tree, never exposed to sun or wind. He had dark hair falling, as fine-spun and straight as silk, across his brow, and his long fingers were curled over the arms of the chair, almost clinging to it, and the desperate clutch of those hands told a silent story of pain.

Magnus had seen portraits like this before, the last images of the lost. He could tell even across the years how much effort it had cost the boy to sit for that portrait, for the comfort of loved ones who would live after he was gone.

His pallid face had the distant look of one who had already taken too many steps along the path to death for him to be recalled. Magnus thought of James Herondale, burning up with too much light, too much love, too much, too much—while the boy in the portrait was as lovely as a dying poet, with the fragile beauty of a candle about to gutter out.

On the ragged wallpaper that might once have been green and that had mutated to a grayish-green color, like a sea flooded with waste, were words written in the same dark brown as the stains on Tatiana's dress. Magnus had to admit to himself what that color was: blood that had been spilled years since and yet never washed clean.

The wallpaper was hanging off the walls in tatters. Magnus could make out only a word here and there on the remaining pieces: PITY, REGRET, INFERNAL.

The last sentence in the series was still legible. It read, MAY GOD HAVE MERCY ON OUR SOULS. Beneath this, written not in blood but cut through the wallpaper into the wall by what Magnus suspected was a different hand, were the words, GOD HAS NO MERCY AND NOR WILL I.

Tatiana sank into an armchair, its upholstery worn and stained by the years, and Grace knelt at her adoptive mother's side on the grimy floor. She knelt daintily, delicately, her skirts billowing around her like the petals of a flower. Magnus supposed that it must have been a habit with her to come to rest in filth, and rise from it to all outward appearance radiantly pure.

"To business, then, madam," said Magnus, and he added silently to himself, *To leaving this house as soon as possible.* "Tell me exactly why you have need of my fabulous and unsurpassed powers, and what you would have me do."

"You can already see, I trust," said Tatiana, "that my Grace is in no need of spells to enhance her natural charms."

Magnus looked at Grace, who was gazing at her hands

linked in her lap. Perhaps she was already using spells. Perhaps she was simply beautiful. Magic or nature, they were much the same thing to Magnus.

"I'm sure she is already an enchantress in her own right."

Grace said nothing, only glanced up at him from under her lashes. It was a demurely devastating look.

"I want something else from you, warlock. I want you," Tatiana said, slowly and distinctly, "to go out into the world and kill me five Shadowhunters. I will tell you how it is to be done, and I will pay you most handsomely."

Magnus was so astonished, he honestly believed he must have heard her incorrectly. "Shadowhunters?" he repeated. "Kill?"

"Is my request so very strange? I have no love for the Shadowhunters."

"But, my dear madam, you *are* a Shadowhunter."

Tatiana Blackthorn folded her hands in her lap. "I am no such thing."

Magnus stared at her for a long moment. "Ah," he said. "I beg your pardon. Uh, would it be terribly uncivil of me to inquire what you do believe yourself to be? Do you think that you are a lamp shade?"

"I do not find your levity amusing."

Magnus's tone was hushed as he said, "I beg your pardon again. Do you believe yourself to be a pianoforte?"

"Hold your tongue, warlock, and do not talk of matters about which you know *nothing*." Tatiana's hands were clenched suddenly, curled as tight as claws in the skirt of her once-bright dress. The note of real agony in her voice was enough to silence Magnus, but she continued. "A Shadowhunter is a warrior. A Shadowhunter is born and trained to be a hand of God upon this earth, wiping it free of evil. That is what our legends say. That is what my father taught me, but my father taught me other things too. He decreed that I would not be trained as a Shadowhunter. He told me that was not my place, that my place in life was to be the dutiful daughter of a warrior, and in time the helpmeet of a noble warrior and the mother of warriors who would carry on the glory of the Shadowhunters for another generation."

Tatiana made a sweeping gesture to the words on the walls, the stains on the floor.

"Such glory," she said, and laughed bitterly. "My father and my family were disgraced, and my husband was torn apart in front of my eyes—torn apart. I had one child, my beautiful boy, my Jesse, but he could not be trained to be a warrior. He was always so weak, so sickly. I begged them not to put the runes on him—I was certain that would kill him—but the Shadowhunters held me back and held him down as they burned the Marks into his flesh. He screamed and screamed. We all thought he would die then, but he did not. He held on for me, for his mama, but their cruelty damned him. Each year he grew sicker and weaker until it was too late. He was sixteen when they told me he could not live."

Her hands moved restlessly as she spoke, from her gesture at the walls to plucking at her gown dyed with old, old blood. She touched her arms as if they still hurt where she had been held back by the Shadowhunters, and she toyed with a large ornate locket that hung around her neck. She opened and closed it, the tarnished metal gleaming between her fingers, and Magnus thought he saw a glimpse of a ghastly portrait. Her son again?

He looked toward the picture on the wall, the pale young face, and calculated how old a child of Rupert Blackthorn's must have been when the man had died twenty-five years before. If Jesse Blackthorn had died when he was sixteen then the boy must have been dead for nine years, but perhaps a mother's mourning never ended.

"I am aware that you have suffered greatly, Mrs. Blackthorn," said Magnus, as gently as he was able. "But instead of some plot of vengeance through the senseless slaughter of Shadowhunters, consider that there are many Shadowhunters who desire nothing more than to help you, and to ease your pain."

"Indeed? Of whom do you speak? William Herondale"— and in Tatiana's mouth hatred dripped from every syllable of Will's name—"sneered at me because all I did was scream as my beloved died, but tell me, what else could I have done? What else had I ever been taught to do?" Tatiana's eyes were huge and poison-green, eyes with enough pain in them to eat away at a world and devour a soul. "Can you tell me, warlock? Could William Herondale tell me?

Can anyone tell me what I should have done, when I did everything I was ever asked to do? My husband is dead, my father is dead, my brothers are lost, my home was stolen, and the Nephilim had no power to save my son. I was everything I was ever asked to be, and as my reward my life was burned to ash. Do not speak to me of easing my pain. My pain is all that I have left. Do not speak to me of being a Shadowhunter. I am not one of them. I refuse to be."

"Very well, madam. You have made your anti-Shadowhunter position amply clear," said Magnus. "What I do not know is why you think I will help you get what you want."

Magnus was many things, but he had never been a fool. The death of a few Shadowhunters was not an aim in itself. If that were all she wanted, she would not have needed to go to Magnus.

The only reason she could have to go to a warlock

was if she wanted to use those deaths, to alchemize Shadowhunter lives into magic for a spell. It would be the darkest of dark spells, and the fact that Tatiana knew of it told Magnus this was not the first time she had turned to dark magic.

What Tatiana Blackthorn, whose pain had eaten away at her like a wolf inside her breast, wanted from dark magic, Magnus did not know. He did not want to know what she had done with power in the past, and he certainly did not want her to have power that could be cataclysmic now.

Tatiana frowned a little puzzled frown that made her look like Benedict Lightwood's spoiled and cosseted daughter again.

"For money, of course."

"You imagine I would kill five people, and leave untold power in your hands," said Magnus, "for money?"

Tatiana waved a hand. "Oh, don't try to drive the price

up by aping your betters and pretending that you have any morals or tender feelings, demon spawn. Name a higher sum and be done with it. The hours of the night are precious to me, and I wish to waste no further time on one such as you."

It was the casualness with which she spoke that was so chilling. Mad though Tatiana might have been, here she was not raving or bitter. She was simply working from the facts as Shadowhunters knew them: that a Downworlder must be so entirely corrupt that she did not even dream he had a heart.

Of course, of course, the vast majority of the Shadowhunters thought of him as something less than human, and as far below the children of the Angel as apes were below men. He might sometimes be useful, but he was a creature to be despised, used but then discarded, his touch avoided because it was unclean.

He had been very useful to Will Herondale, after all. Will had not come to him searching for a friend but a convenient source of magic. Even the best Shadowhunters were not so different from the rest.

"Let me say to you what I said once, in an entirely different context, to Catherine the Great," Magnus declared. "My dear lady, you cannot afford me, and also, please leave that horse alone. Good night."

He made a bow and then made his way, with some speed, out of the room. As the door shut with a snap, he heard Tatiana's voice snapping to match it: "Go after him!"

He was not surprised to hear soft footsteps pattering after him down the stairs. Magnus turned from the front door and met Grace's eyes.

Her footfalls were as light as a child's, but she did not look like a child. In that porcelain-pure face her eyes were gray hollows, deep alluring lakes with sirens in their depths. She met Magnus's eyes with a level gaze, and Magnus was reminded once again of Camille.

It was remarkable that a girl who looked no more than sixteen could rival a centuries-old vampire for self-possession. She had not had time to freeze past caring. *There must*, Magnus thought, *be something behind all this ice.*

"You will not return upstairs, I see," Grace said. "You want no part of Mama's plan."

It was not a question, and she did not sound shocked or curious. It did not seem unthinkable to her, then, that Magnus might have scruples. Perhaps the girl had qualms of conscience herself, but she was shut up here in this dark house with a madwoman, nothing but bitterness poured into her ears from dusk to daybreak. Little wonder if she was different from other girls.

Magnus felt regret suddenly for the way he had

shuddered back from Grace. She was not much more than a child, after all, and nobody knew better than he what it was like to be judged and shunned. He reached out to touch her arm. "Do you have somewhere else to go?" Magnus asked her.

"Somewhere else?" said Grace. "We reside mainly in Idris."

"What I mean is, would she let you leave? Do you need help?"

Grace moved with such speed that it was as if she were a bolt of lightning wrapped in muslin, the long gleaming blade flying from her skirts to her hand. She held the glittering point against Magnus's chest, over his heart.

Here was a Shadowhunter, Magnus thought. Tatiana had learned something from the mistakes of her father. She'd had the girl trained.

"I am no prisoner here."

"No?" Magnus asked. "Then what are you?"

Grace's awful, awe-inspiring eyes narrowed. They were glittering like the steel, and were, Magnus was sure, no less deadly. "I am my mother's blade."

Shadowhunters often died young, and left children behind to be raised by others. That was nothing unusual. It was natural that such a ward, taken into a Shadowhunter's home, would think of and speak to their guardian as a parent. Magnus had thought nothing of it. Yet now it occurred to him that a child might be so grateful to be taken in that her loyalty would be fierce, that a girl raised by Tatiana Blackthorn might not wish for rescue. She might wish for nothing more than the fulfillment of her mother's dark plans.

"Are you threatening me?" Magnus said softly.

"If you do not intend to help us," she said, "then leave this house. Dawn is coming."

"I am not a vampire," Magnus said. "I shall not disappear with the light."

"You will if I kill you before the sun comes up," said Grace. "Who would miss one warlock?"

And she smiled, a wild smile that reminded him again of Camille. That potent blend of beauty and cruelty. He had fallen victim to it himself. He could only imagine again, with growing horror, what the effect would have been on James Herondale, a gentle boy who had been reared to believe that love, too, was gentle. James had given his heart to this girl, Magnus thought, and Magnus knew well enough from Edmund and Will what it meant when a Herondale gave his heart away. It was not a gift that could be returned.

Tessa, Will, and Jem had raised James in love, and had surrounded him with love and the goodness it could produce. But they had given him no armor against the evil. They had wrapped his heart in silks and velvet, and then he had given it to Grace Blackthorn, and she had spun for it a cage of razor wire and broken glass, burned it to bits, and blown away the remains, another layer of ashes in this place of beautiful horrors.

Magnus waved a hand behind his back, then stepped away from Grace's blade, away through the magically open door.

"You will tell no one of what my mother asked of you tonight," said Grace. "Or I will ensure your destruction."

"I believe you think you could," Magnus breathed. She was terrible and brilliant, like the light shining off the edge of a razor. "Oh, and by the way? I suspect that if James Herondale had known I was coming here, he would have sent his regards."

Grace lowered her sword, nothing more. Its point rested gently on the ground. Her hand did not shake, and her lashes screened her eyes. "What do I care for James Herondale?" she asked.

"I thought you might. After all, a blade does not get to choose where it is pointed."

Grace looked up. Her eyes were still, deep pools, entirely unruffled.

"A blade does not care," she told him.

Magnus turned and made his way past tangles of black roses and undergrowth down toward the rusted gates. He looked back at the manor only once, saw the wreck of what had been grand and gracious, and saw a curtain fluttering in a window high above, and the suggestion of a face. He wondered who was watching him go.

He could warn Downworlders to steer clear of Tatiana and her endeavors. No matter what the price offered, no Downworlder would fail to listen to a warning against one of the Nephilim. Tatiana would raise no dark magic.

Magnus could do that much, but he did not see a way to help James Herondale. Grace and Tatiana might have cast a spell on him, Magnus supposed. He would not put it past either of them, but he could not see why they would. What possible role could James Herondale have to play in whatever dark plot they were hatching? More likely the boy had simply fallen prey to her charms. Love was love; there was no spell to cure a broken heart that did not also destroy that heart's capacity for love forever.

And there was no reason for Magnus to tell Will and Tessa what he had learned. James's feelings for Grace were his secret to keep. Magnus had told the boy he would never betray his secrets; he had sworn it. He had never betrayed Will's confidence, and he would not betray James's now. What good would it do Will and Tessa, to know the name of their son's pain and still have no remedy for it?

He thought once more of Camille, and how it had hurt

him to learn the truth about her, how he had struggled like a man crawling over knives not to know it, and finally, with even greater pain, had been forced to accept it.

Magnus did not take such suffering lightly, but even mortals did not die of broken hearts. No matter how cruel Grace had been, he told himself, James would heal. Even though he was a Herondale.

He opened the gates with his hands, thorns scratching his flesh, and he remembered again his first sight of Grace and the feeling he'd had of being faced with a predator. She was very different from Tessa, who had always steadied and anchored Will, softened his eyes into humor and his lips to gentleness.

It would be ironic, Magnus thought, terribly and cruelly ironic, for one Herondale to be saved by love, and another Herondale damned by it.

He tried to shake off both the memory of Tessa and

Will and the echo of Tatiana's condemning words. He had promised Tessa that he would return, but now he found all he wanted to do was escape. He did not want to care what Shadowhunters thought of him. He did not want to care what would become of them or their children.

He had offered help to three Shadowhunters this night. One of them had replied that he was beyond help, one had asked him to commit murder, and one had pointed a blade at him.

His relationship of mutual distant tolerance with the Whitelaws of the New York Institute seemed suddenly alluring. He was part of Downworld New York, and would have it no other way. He was glad he had left London. He discovered in himself a pang for New York and its brighter lights, and fewer broken hearts.

"Where to?" asked the driver.

Magnus thought of the ship from Southampton to

New York, of standing on the deck of the boat, letting the sea air wash him clean of the musty air of London. He said, "I believe I am going home."